Make Believe It's Y...

The adventures of

THUMBELINA

starring you

by Margaret and Carson Davidson

illustrated by Yuri Salzman

SCHOLASTIC INC.

New York Toronto London Auckland Sydney

These tales of magic and make-believe are dedicated to Bill Haber, who has his own special brand of magic.

ISBN 0-590-42529-3

Copyright © 1987 by Margaret & Carson Davidson.
All rights reserved. Published by Scholastic Inc.

MAKE BELIEVE IT'S YOU is a trademark of Scholastic Inc.
Art Direction by Diana Hrisinko.

12 11 10 9 8 7 6 5 4 3   3/9

Printed in the U.S.A.   28
First Scholastic Printing, May 1987

WAIT! READ THIS FIRST:

Most books are about other people. This book is about *you*. What happens to you depends on what you decide to do. Do you want to meet a dragon? Or a magician? Or a handsome prince? There are many adventures waiting for you in this book.

But there is one thing you must remember. Do not read this book from the first page to the last. If you do, the story won't make sense. Instead, start on page one and read until you come to your first choice. Then turn to the page you decide on and see what happens. Each choice will lead you to another choice — until your adventure comes to an end. Then it is time to go back and start all over again.

Have fun!

It's night outside, and your room is lit softly by
candles. You are standing in front of a mirror
looking at yourself. Am I pretty? you wonder.

You're not sure. But you do know one thing —
you're small. Very small. You're no bigger, in
fact, than most people's thumb. Which is why
your mother named you Thumbelina.

Now she comes bustling into the room. "Time
for bed," she says. So you climb into your bed.
It's a walnut shell, polished to a bright brown.
Your mattress is stuffed with violet petals. Your
blanket is the leaf of a rose.

You drift off to sleep. Before long you're having
a happy dream. But then something strange happens. A big frog hops in through the window. She
comes right up to your bed and peers at you with
her beady eyes.

"Well, well," she croaks, "what a lovely wife
for my son."

Then she picks up your walnut-shell bed and
starts off — with you still in it!

*If you wake up and leap out of the shell, turn
to* **page 16.**

*If you sleep right through the whole thing, turn
to* **page 68.**

2   "Don't bother with the magician," you tell the Prince. "I don't want to get any bigger."

This makes him very angry, and he starts shouting. So you decide to leave right away.

You say a warm good-bye to the Prince's mother. After all — frog or Queen — you like her a lot. Then you start on your way again.

Oh, I do want to go home, you think as you walk along. If only I can find the way.

It isn't easy. As a matter of fact it takes you days and days. By the time you see the little cottage in the distance, you've never been so tired.

"Thumbelina!" cries your mother, when she sees you. "Oh, Thumbelina, you've come back! I thought you'd left me forever."

You tell her about some of your adventures. She's very impressed. "So young, and already you know so much more about the world than I do. It's wonderful!"

"All the same, it's really nice to be back home."

"Well, my dear," says your mother, "I have some news for you, too. When I thought you were never coming home again, I went back to the witch."

"The witch?"

Go on to the next page.

"Yes, don't you remember? I told you about her. She's the one who gave me the magic seed. The seed that grew into the flower, with you inside of it."

"Oh, yes, I remember now. Why did you go back to her?"

"I wanted to get another tiny child, just like you. And she gave me one more seed."

You jump up and clap your hands. "So there's another one like me? How wonderful! Oh, where is she?"

Your mother takes you into the next room. Sitting there is a girl — and she's as small as you are!

Suddenly you are filled with happiness. For you know you have finally found the one thing that's been missing from your life — a best friend to share things with.

THE END

4   You keep looking at the frog. And he keeps looking just like a frog. Oh, well, you think. Nobody's right all the time.

Soon, though, you notice that the two frogs are staring at *you*. What's the matter? you wonder. Is my face dirty? Or maybe it's my dress?

You look down — and then you realize. The kiss did work, after all. Only not quite the way you expected. The frog didn't turn into a prince — *you* turned into a frog!

Something like this takes a little getting used to. You sit down and try to think it out. After a while your friend comes over and puts her webbed paw on your shoulder. "Look, you shouldn't take it so hard. The end of the world it's not."

"I know. It's just sort of a surprise."

She nods. "But being a frog isn't so bad. Matter of fact, I've always kind of liked it. Just keep thinking — green is great, green is grand, green is gorgeous! That ought to help."

"I'll . . . I'll try," you tell her.

"And what I'll do is, I'll take you around and introduce you to some nice frogs. You'll like them. And they'll like you — that I can guarantee."

Go on to the next page.

She's right. Everyone likes you. They think 5 you're the prettiest frog they've ever seen. Also the smartest. You're invited everywhere, of course. And you have a wonderful time.

Then one day you meet a special frog named Fernando. He likes to quote poetry. And at night he comes around with a guitar and sings outside your window. Who could resist such a romantic type?

You can't. "And just think," you tell him one day. "If I hadn't kissed the wrong frog, I'd never, ever have met the right one."

THE END

6   So you marry the mole, and you live with him all winter. He's just as dull as you thought he would be. His house is just as dark as you thought it would be. And you're just as unhappy as you thought you would be.

Then spring comes. One night, after the mole has fallen asleep, you sneak out of the house. As soon as you get outside you clap your hands with delight. For the air is filled with fireflies. They are lighting up the whole meadow with their blinking, twinkling lanterns.

Suddenly you have an idea. You call some of the fireflies over. "I'm having a party tomorrow night," you say. "Everyone's invited, so tell all your friends."

"Great!" say the fireflies. "Is there anything we can bring?"

That's when you get your second idea.

"Yes," you answer, "bring flowers!"

Your husband isn't happy when the fireflies start to arrive the next evening. Not happy at all.

"Tell them to go away!" he snaps. "Tell them to take their awful lights and their awful flowers and get out of here!"

"I'm afraid it's too late," you tell him. "I don't know how to get them out. You could try, if you want to."

Go on to the next page.

But of course a mole is too slow to catch fireflies,
so *that* doesn't work. And the party goes on. Your husband just sits around, making gloomy noises.

Before long, though, you notice that he's talking with one of the older, quieter fireflies. A few minutes later he's laughing at a joke one of the younger fireflies made. Soon *he* tells a joke. It's not very funny — but everyone laughs politely.

By the end of the evening, the mole actually smells some of the flowers. "Well, well," he says, "so that's what flowers smell like. Not bad."

The next morning he turns to you. "Hummmph," he says.

"Yes, dear?"

"Just clearing my throat."

"Oh," you say. "I thought you were going to say something."

"Well," he finally bursts out, "all that light in here last night — it was sort of . . . sort of. . . ."

"Sort of what?"

"Well, interesting."

"I'm glad you liked it."

"I didn't say I *liked* it," the mole answers quickly. "I just said it was interesting."

After another small silence he asks, "Is . . . is the sun something like that?"

"Oh, yes," you tell him, "only nicer."

Turn to **page 8.**

8   "Hmmmmmm. Well, in that case — just in the interest of science, of course — I think we ought to go and have a look at it."

From that day on, he's a new mole. "We've got to brighten this place up," he says, looking around the house. "We'll put in a couple of windows over there. And a skylight in the corner. Maybe a sunporch, off the bedroom."

"Oh, that would be wonderful," you say. "And I think you're wonderful, too!"

"Hmmmmph," he says. "Of course I am. Everyone knows that."

Oh, well, you think, you can't make an old mole into an *entirely* new one — not all at once.

But he keeps on changing. A few days later he says, "It's kind of drab in here, don't you think? What we need are flowers to brighten the place up. Lots and lots of flowers! Let's take a walk right now and bring back a whole bunch."

"Let's." And you slip your hand into his paw.

Before you've gone very far, you hear a bird overhead. "Hi!" he calls down to you. "It's me! I've come back for a visit." And there he is — your friend, the swallow.

"I'm so glad to see you!" you say to him. "Come and meet my husband."

"Your husband?! I thought he hated — "

Go on to the next page.

"Well, he doesn't now," you say quickly. "And I'm sure the two of you are going to be great friends."

"Friends?" says the bird. He sounds doubtful.

But the mole just slaps him on the back. "Of course we are!" he says. "Any friend of the wife's is a friend of mine. Tell me, how would you like to come home with us for a bite to eat?"

"I'd like that," says the swallow, "very much."

Before dinner is over, they're talking like old, old friends. And your husband has still another new idea. "Fall will be here soon," he says. "Do you suppose you could. . . ."

"Yes?" the swallow asks.

"Well," the mole continues, smiling shyly at you. "I thought it might be nice if I took Thumbelina south for the winter . . . as a kind of second honeymoon. Everyone knows it's the perfect place for one. Yes, everyone knows that. So would it be asking too much of you. . . ."

"I'll fly you there!" cries the swallow happily. "I'm so glad you want to go."

"We have Thumbelina to thank for that," says your husband. "She's the one who made me into a different mole."

Then the three of you laugh, and you all say together, "Everyone knows that!"

THE END

10   You know exactly what to do. You close your eyes. Then you try to remember how you felt when you first saw your parents. They looked so dried-up and dead.

It was the most terrible sadness you've ever known. Tears come to your eyes, just thinking about it.

Quickly you put a finger to your cheek and lift off a tear. Then you throw the tear back over your shoulder.

An instant later that single drop touches the terrible bird of fire. There's a sound like red-hot metal being plunged into water. There's a cloud of steam. And after that . . . nothing. The flaming bird is simply gone. Gone forever.

Soon Amadeus carries you and your parents far away from the Valley Most Deep. "But where can we go?" your mother asks. "I've spent my whole life in that valley. I don't know anywhere else."

"Neither do I," says your father.

But you do. You lean down and whisper in Amadeus's ear. He changes direction, and a few hours later you land in a flower garden next to a small cottage.

Go on to the next page.

A woman comes to the door. Then she gives a glad cry. "Thumbelina! It's Thumbelina! Oh, my child, you've come back to me!" It's your adoptive mother.

You love your real parents with all your heart. But this is the woman who raised you since birth, and you love her just as much. So now all of you settle down together.

And that's a really happy ending.

THE END

12   You have to wait until tomorrow noon. So you lie down on the ground and close your eyes. But you can't fall asleep. You're too hot. And too worried. Besides, you seem to be lying on some rocks.

You reach down to push them out of the way. Then you realize they're not rocks. They're the two jewels Wilma the Witch gave you.

You pull them out of your pocket and look at them. The witch said that one of them could help you. But which one?

At first you can't tell. But then you notice that high overhead there's a full moon. Next to the flames in the valley, it looks almost blue.

Blue. . . . You study the blue jewel in your hand. A soft blue light seems to be coming from inside it. A soft blue *cool* light. . . .

And suddenly you know exactly what to do. You raise the blue stone toward that full moon. And right away it grows brighter. The stone is soaking up the blue, blue light.

Slowly, the moon moves across the sky. And you move with it, always holding the jewel in its light. At last, the moon sets. By then the gem is blazing like a blue, blue lighthouse in the night. Finally you can lie down and go to sleep.

Go on to the next page.

When you wake, it's almost noon on the longest day of the year. You stand with the blue jewel in your hand — waiting for the path to appear. Then you happen to turn away for a moment. When you turn back, the path is there!

You're scared. You've never been so scared in your life. But you know that you must follow that path down into the valley. So you take a deep breath and start.

Flames are everywhere. They crackle and hiss and lick at you from every side. But you hold out the jewel. Its cool, blue light touches the flames nearest you . . . and they fall back. Again you hold out the jewel . . . and again the flames fall back.

With your jewel, you carve out a narrow path of safety through the flames. Now you are deep in the valley itself. You stop for a moment to look around.

What an awful place, you think. There's no grass. No flowers. No trees. Everything has been burned bare.

Suddenly a shrill scream cuts through the air. You look around wildly. High up on a rock there's a bird — the biggest bird you've ever seen. And, like everything else in this horrible place, it's on fire!

Turn to **page 15.**

The bird screams again. Then, flapping its fiery wings, it starts toward you.

Its beak is open. Its claws are out, reaching for you. Sparks pour from its eyes. And every one of its feathers is trailing a stream of fire!

You have just seconds to escape! So you do the only thing you can think of — you dive to the ground. Then you wedge yourself between two rocks. Maybe this terrible burning bird won't be able to get at you there.

If this plan works, turn to **page 60.**

If it doesn't, turn to **page 65.**

16   You scramble out of the shell and run as fast as you can. That's not very fast, of course, because you're so small. And the frog's right behind you!

Ahead of you is a mouse hole — too small for this big frog. You'll be safe, if you can only get to it. But can you? You feel her hot breath on the back of your neck. You run faster and faster. . . . At last you dive headfirst into the hole!

The frog skids to a stop and peers in. "So, my pretty," she says. "You got away this time. But mark my words — I'll be back. I won't rest until you are my son's bride."

There's no more sleep for you that night. As soon as morning comes you tell your mother what happened. "What can I do?" you ask. "I'm sure she'll try again."

"Thumbelina," your mother answers, "you know that you were adopted."

You nod. Your mother has told you this many times.

"Well," she goes on, "I didn't tell you the whole story. I was waiting until you were older. You see, I wanted a baby very, very much. I wanted a baby so much I went to an old witch and asked her for one."

"A witch?!" you cry. "But witches are wicked!"

Go on to the next page.

"Oh, no, not this one. She's a very good witch. And what she did was give me a seed."

"A seed?"

"Yes," your mother continues. "She told me to plant it in a flowerpot. And soon a beautiful flower grew out of it. It looked like a tulip, with its petals folded tightly together."

"A tulip?" you whisper.

"Yes. Then the flower popped open. And there you were, lying inside of it — just as beautiful as you are today."

Your mother takes your hand. "Thumbelina, I have loved you from the moment I lifted you out of that flower. But I can't help you now. So I think you should go and see Wilma. She's the good witch."

Your mother tells you how to get to Wilma the Witch's house, and you set off. The trip wouldn't seem far to most people. But you're not most people, of course, so it takes you three days to get there. All the while you worry. You've never heard of a good witch before.

But as soon as you see Wilma you know everything's going to be all right. She's round all over and has twinkling eyes. She looks just like someone's grandmother. Quickly you tell her about the frog.

Turn to **page 18.**

18 "Oh, dear, oh, dear," says Wilma. "That will never do. We'll just have to get you away from here for a while. Oh, I know! We'll send you on a Quest!"

"A Quest? What's that?"

"Oh, you young people don't know anything these days," scolds the witch. "A Quest is where you go far, far away to find something very, very important."

"Important?" you say. "Like what?"

"That's for you to decide, my dear. It's your Quest, after all."

You think as hard as you can. "Well . . ." you say finally, "I'd like to — yes, I'd like to find my parents. My real parents."

"Good," says the witch.

"And . . . and then I'd like to find the man I'm going to love."

The good witch shakes her head. "That's two Quests, Thumbelina, not one. I'm afraid you'll have to choose."

If you choose to go looking for your parents, turn to **page 45.**

If you decide to find the man you're going to love, turn to **page 32.**

You have a wonderful time in the meadow.
There's plenty to eat — nuts and berries and honey. Every morning there's fresh dew to drink. There are lots of other meadow creatures for you to be friends with. And when you get tired, you just lean back against a rose-bud pillow and let the birds' sweet songs lull you to sleep.

You *are* warned that this good life won't last forever. An ant scurries past, carrying some grain. "You'd better find a snug place to live," she scolds. "And begin to store some food for winter." But you just laugh and go on having a good time.

That's too bad, for you find out all too soon that the ant was right. Autumn comes, and then winter. It begins to snow. Your thin dress was not made for this sort of weather. You shiver with each new blast of wind that howls down from the north.

I'll surely freeze to death, you think. Or starve. Oh, there's no hope for me at all.

But then your luck turns. A kind-hearted mouse pokes her head out of a hole in the ground and sees you.

"You poor dear," she says. "You can't stay out there. Come inside, come inside — do."

Turn to **page 20.**

20   You don't have to be asked twice. As soon as you warm up a little, the mouse gives you a big meal of fried acorns and roots. Then she asks if you'd like to stay for the winter. "But you must earn your way, my dear, by keeping my place nice and tidy." So you and the mouse settle down in her snug little home.

One night, about a week later, the two of you have a visitor. He's a big, sleek mole. He's nice enough, but he has strong opinions about everything. Like all moles, he's almost blind, and he's lived his whole life underground.

"The sun is a terrible thing," he says. "It's far too bright. Everyone knows that. And flowers are terrible, as well. All they do is smell. Everyone knows that, too."

Later, after he has gone home, the mouse says, "I think the mole would make a perfect husband for you. He's so rich. Why, his house is ten times as big as mine. And did you see that fine fur coat he was wearing?"

Husband?! Why does everyone want me to get married all of a sudden? you think. And to such strange types!

Go on to the next page.

For the mole may be a good creature, but you don't like him much. He's so sure he's *right* about everything. And he hates all the things you love best — like the bright sun overhead and the beautiful flowers growing out of the earth.

A week later the mole comes visiting again. He has dug a tunnel between his house and yours. "You must use it to visit me," he says. "Won't you come now?"

So you and the mouse follow him into the tunnel. It turns and twists. Then, around one of the bends, you come upon the body of a dead swallow.

"Pay no attention to him," says the mole. "When I was digging, I got too close to the surface, and *that* fell through. Totally selfish of him, I thought. But I didn't let him stop me. Not *me*. I just patched up the ceiling and dug around him."

"Oh, that was so clever of you," says the mouse.

"I know," says the mole.

You can't help feeling bad. You love birds. They look so pretty in the sky. And they sing so sweetly. Why, you think sadly, this might be one of the very birds that sang me to sleep last summer.

Turn to **page 22.**

The mole's high, squeaky voice breaks into these sad thoughts. "Birds! Stupid creatures. Not a brain in their heads. Everyone knows that. Well, come along."

The mole's house *is* grand. But you don't like it any better than you like him. It's far too full of *things*. There are so many chairs and tables and couches that you can hardly move around. You're very glad when the visit finally comes to an end and you're back in your own bed again.

But you find you can't sleep. You keep thinking about that poor swallow. You know he's dead. But you hate to think of him lying out there in that cold, cold tunnel.

Finally you get up and gather a little soft wool you've seen in the back of a closet. You creep into the tunnel and tuck your wool all around the bird. "There," you say softly, as you lay your face against the bird's body. "Even if you're dead, you deserve to be warm."

Go on to the next page.

But then you jump back! For something inside the bird is going *thump . . . thump . . . thump. . . .*

It's the bird's heart. He wasn't dead at all — only half frozen. And the warmth of your wool has brought him back to life!

But what do you do now? How can you keep the swallow alive?

If you think you'd better get some help with this problem, turn to **page 50.**

If you decide you'll have to do it by yourself, turn to **page 41.**

24   You look up at the Mountain Most High. It looks more like a sheer wall of ice than a mountain, you think. How can I possibly get to the city on top of that?

But then you see a path, clinging to the side of the mountain. So you start climbing. The path isn't just steep. It's slippery. Again and again you slither and slide and almost fall. But somehow you keep going.

After what seems like hours and hours, you notice that the air is getting warmer. The ice on the path seems to be thinner. Finally, you are walking over bare patches of earth with bits of grass growing on them.

By the time you get to the top, there's no ice at all. Flowers are growing everywhere. You don't stop to pick any, though, for right in front of you is the city in the sky.

But how can you get in? A wall surrounds it. Set in the wall is a gate. You try to push it open, but it's locked. You knock. Nothing happens. You knock again. Still nothing. You shout. Silence is your only answer.

Go on to the next page.

Then you notice the color of the gate. It's bright, bright blue. The same color as your blue jewel. The same color. . . . And this gives you an idea. You take out the jewel and tap the gate with it three times. Before you can lower your arm, the gate is open.

You walk into the city. The streets are narrow and winding. You turn corner after corner — looking for the people who live here. At first there is no one. Finally, up ahead, you see an old woman.

Then you blink with surprise. Why, she's a *little* old woman, you think . . . no bigger than I am!

You rush up to her. "Please, can you tell me where I am?"

"Where? Why, in Lilliput, of course. But hurry along now. He's waiting, and you're going to be late!"

"Late? Late for what? How can I be late for something when I don't even know where I am? And who's waiting?"

But the old woman just frowns crossly and says, "Get along with you, now! It's the red door. Far end of town." Then she dashes off.

Turn to **page 26.**

26   Because you can't think of anything else to do, you walk on. A few minutes later you see a man. And *he's* not any bigger than you are, either.

"Please," you ask, "can you tell me where I am?"

But all he says is, "No time to talk! Hurry, girl! Red door — far end of town!" Then he, too, is gone.

Again you walk on through the streets of Lilliput. And you notice that all the doors are black. But finally, at the very far end of town, you come to a house which is much bigger than the others. And its door is a blazing bright red.

This time you know what to do. You take out your red jewel and tap the door three times. It opens . . . you walk through . . . and suddenly you're in a palace. A very large, very beautiful palace.

You walk down one corridor after another until you come to a big room. At the far end of the room is a throne. And standing in front of the throne is a very handsome man wearing a crown. You think he must be King of wherever this is.

There are many other people there — all dressed in their finest clothes. And the room is decorated with streamers and bows and big bunches of flowers.

Turn to **page 28.**

You can see that a wedding is about to take place. But who's getting married? It must be someone very important.

Just then two servants rush up and pull you forward. They lead you up to the man wearing the crown. Then suddenly you know who is getting married. You are.

"I don't understand . . . I don't know you, do I?" you whisper.

The King shakes his head. "No, and I don't know you. But I knew you were coming. We all knew you were coming on this, the shortest day of the year." And then he smiles a very warm smile.

"I feel as though I'm in the middle of a dream," you say, smiling back.

"That's the way I feel, too," says the King. "A very *good* dream. Shall we let it continue?"

You nod. That's just what you want to do. For you know now that your quest is over. So you are married then and there — married to a man you've never seen before.

One year later your first child is born. And what do you name her? Wilma, of course. (Her middle initial is also W — for *Witch* — but you don't tell anyone that.)

And you live happily ever after. Of course.

THE END

The swallow tells you to go — he'll be all right.
But you know that he still needs a lot of help. So, very sadly, you say good-bye to Hop o' my Thumb. "I'll never forget you, and all you did for us."

"I'll never forget you, either, Thumbelina," answers Hop o' my Thumb. And then he is gone.

For weeks you nurse the swallow. You feed him and keep him safe. And little by little he grows stronger. Soon he will be able to take care of himself. Then what will you do?

You find that more and more often you think about Hop o' my Thumb. You think about how brave he was. And how much fun, too. I wish he hadn't gone, you think.

And then . . . then one morning you see a familiar figure — far, far away. A figure that comes rushing toward you. It's Hop o' my Thumb. He's come back!

"I couldn't get you out of my mind," he says. "And the more I thought of you, the more I knew that I wanted you to become my wife — and share the rest of my life. Will you, Thumbelina?"

You know you're going to say yes.

Turn to **page 30.**

"There's just one thing I must tell you," Hop adds. "When I came back here, I gave up my house, my land, everything. I don't have a thing to my name but a pair of speedy boots. If you marry me, you'll marry a poor man."

"I'm poor, too," you say. "We'll be poor together."

And so the two of you are married. You settle down in a little cottage in the southern lands. And you're poor together.

But not for long. The King of the Southern Lands happens to be fighting a war. All the battles are very far away. So he doesn't get news of them for days and days. This makes him very unhappy.

One day Hop o' my Thumb puts on his seven-league boots and goes to the battlefield. It only takes him a minute and a half. He finds out who won the battle that day. And he brings back the news to the King.

This makes him very happy. And when the King is happy, he gives people things. He gives your husband three large rubies that first day. As Hop keeps on bringing back the news, the King keeps giving him more jewels. This adds up, of course. And before long you are very rich.

Go on to the next page.

Then the war ends. For a while Hop and you live quietly. But soon he grows restless and decides to go into business — with his seven-league boots, of course. He announces that he'll go anywhere to find out anything for anyone. He calls this new company "Hop's Seven-League Boots Same-Day News Service."

It's a big success. So you become even richer. But that's not what you like most about Hop's new job — what you like are the stories he brings back to tell you every night. Stories of the strange sights he has seen that day and the even stranger people he has met.

Why, you think happily, as you settle down to listen to still another wonderful story, it's like being married to a whole book of Fairy Tales!

THE END

"I want to find the man I'm going to love," you tell the witch.

"Fine," she says. "But I must warn you, Thumbelina. This Quest will be very hard. You'll have to go far, far away to the farthest northern lands. You will have to keep going until you come to the Mountain Most High. There you will find a cave. Inside it will be the end of your Quest."

"Northern lands . . . Mountain Most High . . . that does sound far."

Because you're so small it takes you much longer than other people to get anywhere. "But I will go," you say. "How will I know when I am there?"

"Ask the Mountain," says Wilma the Witch. "It will tell you."

You nod. "Is there anything I can take along to help me?"

"Ah, you are a clever girl," says the witch. "Yes, there is. Here, take these." She holds out two very large jewels. One is a rich, rich red. The other is a bright, bright blue.

"I can tell you that these are magic jewels," Wilma says. "But that is all I can say about them. You alone will have to figure out which one to use. And when. And how."

Go on to the next page.

"Very well," you say. "Is there anything else **33** you can tell me?"

"Yes, I can tell you this. You must get to the Mountain at just the right time. For you can only find the entrance to the cave exactly at midnight on the shortest day of the year. And then for only sixty seconds."

"One minute a year," you say. "Then that's when I'll be there."

As you start out, you sing a happy song. Up until now you've led such a quiet life. Now something tells you that this Quest is going to be fun!

And it is — at first. Often you make friends with others you meet along the way. One evening it rains really hard. But you don't get wet, because a friendly family of badgers invites you into their snug den. But when they ask you to stay and visit for a while you say no. You know you still have a long, long way to go — and time is passing all too fast.

Every day is shorter than the last. And colder, too. Often an icy wind blows from the north. Then snow begins to fall.

Turn to **page 34.**

This isn't as much fun as it used to be. You're cold. And you're tired. But the shortest day is getting closer all the time. So you just keep plodding on.

Finally, on the last day, you see a steep, steep mountain ahead of you. It's covered with ice. You remember what Wilma the Witch told you to do.

"Is this the place?" you ask. "Have I reached the Mountain Most High?"

Then, soft as a sigh, you hear an answer:

"Yes, yes, wee Thumbelina, yes;
   You're here in time, my dear;
Midnight will bring you full success —
   The entrance will appear."

But do you want to go into that cave? The mountain before you is a sheer wall of ice. It seems to reach almost to the sky. It's very cold, and you know that the cave will be colder still. And darker. Much darker.

Then you happen to look up . . . up to the very top of this mountain of ice. And you see that there is a city there, a city in the sky.

Go on to the next page.

You have a choice to make. Do you want to try climbing up to that city? It might be very dangerous.

Or do you want to wait until midnight and go into the cave? That might be even more dangerous.

If you decide to go on, turn to **page 39.**

If you think the city looks more interesting, turn to **page 24.**

36 When the magician arrives, the Prince points to you. "Make her bigger," he says.

"Bigger. All right, how much bigger?"

"Normal-sized bigger. Like other girls."

"Oh, them," says the magician, and goes to work. He mixes up some powder in a glass of water. He says some words over it. He makes a lot of smoke and a very bad odor. A few seconds later there's a small bang, and there you are — almost as big as the Prince.

"That what you had in mind?" asks the magician.

"It'll do," says the Prince. "You may go." He then begins to make plans for the Grand Wedding — his and yours.

You think it might be fun to be a Princess. But you're not at all sure you want to be married to *this* Prince. He's just as vain now as when he was a frog. More so, in fact. He's always going around the palace singing little songs like:

"Oh, it's great to be a me;
I'm so handsome it's alarming;
People come for miles to see
A Prince so handsome and so charming."

This gets pretty hard to take after a while.

Go on to the next page.

You go and have a talk with the magician. "The Prince," you say, "thinks very highly of himself."

"I know. I've heard his little songs, too," the magician says sourly.

"Well, I can't stand it any more. Is there anything you can do about it?"

"Not a chance. He's my boss, you know."

That stops you for a while. But then you decide to try someone else. Your mother used to tell you about a good witch named Wilma. This witch gave your mother a magic seed. It turned into a flower, and you were in the flower. So maybe Wilma will help you now.

You go back to the old neighborhood. You ask around until you find her house.

"Well, I'm really glad to see you," says Wilma. "Though I must say you're a good deal bigger than I'd expected."

You explain about getting made Prince-sized by the magician. Then you ask her to help you with the Prince's I'm-So-Handsome problem.

"Handsome, eh?" says the witch. She paws through a large book of spells. "Habits . . . hags . . . halibut . . . ah, here we are — handsome." She reads a little more. "Well, this shouldn't be too hard."

Turn to **page 38.**

She mixes up some powder in a glass of water. She says some words over it. She makes a lot of smoke and a very bad odor. A few seconds later, there's a small bang. Then the witch says, "That should about do it. Run along and see how he is by now."

You thank her very much and go back to the palace. The first person you meet is your friend, the Prince's mother.

"You won't believe it!" she exclaims. "*I* don't believe it, and I'm his mother. He's turned nice!"

"He has?"

"Would I lie to you? Suddenly everyone likes him. Even *me*! Imagine that. It's like magic."

"Well, as a matter of fact, it *was* magic." You tell her what you and Wilma the Witch did.

"Aha! First time I met you I said to myself — that girl's no fool. And I was right — you're no fool."

Just then you hear the Prince singing as he walks down the hall. You can't catch much of the song, but the last line goes, "Thumbelina's the prettiest girl in the world."

His mother turns to you. "Did I lie, Thumbelina? So why not marry him? You could do worse."

Being no fool, you do exactly that.

THE END

You remember what the witch said. She told you that the end of your Quest was in the cave. So you decide to stay right where you are.

You also remember something else — the jewels Wilma gave you. You take them from your pocket and look at them. She told you that there was a way to use one of them. But which one? And how?

As you stand in the bright sunlight, you find you're looking more and more at the red stone. There's a soft glow about it. And it feels just a little *warm* in your hand. It seems to be soaking up the sunlight. Suddenly you know what to do.

You hold the red stone up to the sun. You hold it there all day. And it glows redder and redder, until by nightfall it's blazing like fire.

Now all you can do is wait — wait until midnight on this, the shortest day of the year.

Just at twelve o'clock, you hear a small sound behind you. You turn around. When you look back at the wall of ice, the entrance to the cave is there.

You take a deep breath and go inside. You can tell that it's cold, cold, cold. You hardly feel it, though. For the red stone keeps you warm all over. The jewel also gives off a soft light. But beyond its glow there is only inky darkness.

Go on to the next page.

40   As you go deeper and deeper into the cave, you stumble through frozen fields of jagged ice. You climb frozen waterfalls. You slip and slide across frozen lakes. But you keep on going, no matter what. For you know that somewhere ahead of you lies the reason for your Quest.

At last you come to a huge underground room. It's filled with pillars of glittering ice — hundreds and hundreds of them.

You begin to walk between them. Each one looks exactly like the next. But then something catches your eye.

You stop and look more closely. Something is deep inside one of the pillars. Something that looks like . . . like a man! Yes, there *is* someone there — frozen in the middle of the ice!

He must be dead, you think. How could he be alive? It's just not possible. And yet . . . could he be?

You know you can't break that ice. It's as solid as rock. So what can you do? Is there any way to get him out?

If you think of a way that might work, turn to **page 72.**

If you can't, then you'd probably better get out of that cave. So turn back to **page 32** *and make another choice.*

All winter long you stay with the mouse, and
every night you creep out to take care of the
swallow. You bring him food and water. You keep
him warm. And little by little he grows stronger.

Finally spring comes. The swallow is well
enough to fly off into the nearby meadows and
woods. "Won't you come with me, Thumbelina?"
he says. "I could easily carry you on my back."

Oh, you want to go so much! You remember so
clearly how you loved the meadow last summer.
But you also remember how kind the mouse has
been to you.

"I can't just go off and leave her," you say.
"She'd be terribly unhappy."

"Then good-bye, little Thumbelina," says the
bird. "I'll never forget you for saving my life."

You go back into the house. "Come, come,"
says the mouse briskly. "We've got *so* much to
do. And only the summer to do it in."

"Do? Do what?"

"Why, we've got to get you ready for your
wedding."

"Wedding?!" you cry.

"Yes, yes. The mole and I have decided that
the two of you will be married in the fall."

Marry the mole? Oh, no! "I can't," you wail.
"I don't love him!"

Turn to **page 42.**

"That has nothing to do with it," answers the mouse. "He's rich. Now *that's* the kind of thing that matters!"

"But he hates the sun. I love it. He hates flowers. I love them. He even hates the birds. And I'd have to live in the dark for the rest of my life!"

"Oh, you'll get used to it," says the mouse. "And it's for your own good, my dear."

So all summer long, the mouse keeps you busy spinning and weaving and sewing. You make sheets and tablecloths and beautiful dresses. And each new thing you sew is trimmed with fine lace made of spiders' webs. "After all," says the mouse, "the mole will expect it. He's used to the *very* best."

You're kept so busy you hardly have time to go outside. The few times you do, you look for your old friend the bird. But he's never there.

Then — all too soon — your wedding day arrives. You rise very early and slip outside one last time. With a heavy heart you say good-bye to the sun and the flowers. You say good-bye to the wind and the fresh air and all the creatures of the meadows and the woods. For you know that you will almost never see them again, once you are Mrs. Mole.

Go on to the next page.

Now the mouse calls, "Come back inside,
Thumbelina. It's time to dress for your wedding."

You're about to go in. But then you hear something else, and your heart gives a wild leap. For it's the voice of your friend, the swallow. He's come back!

You tell him about your coming marriage. "I'll have to live under the ground for the rest of my life," you say mournfully. "Oh, it's going to be so boring!"

"Why, then, come away with me," says the swallow. "Today I'm going south for the winter. I'm going to a place where the sun shines twice as much as here. The sky seems twice as high. The trees are filled with ripe fruit. The vines are heavy with purple grapes. And the air is always sweet with the smell of flowers."

"Oh, it does sound wonderful," you sigh. "But it would make the mouse feel just awful. And she really thinks this is the best thing for me."

If you decide this is the best thing for you, and besides you don't want to make the mouse so unhappy, turn to **page 6.**

If you want to go with the swallow anyway, turn to **page 58.**

You're pretty sure you do like Hop o' my Thumb. But first you have to ask the bird. Is he really strong enough to be left on his own?

"Oh, yes, I'll be fine," yawns the bird, waking up from his nap. "I've already seen a couple of old friends. They'll take care of me if I need any help. Run along, now!"

So off you go on Hop o' my Thumb's back — fast, as usual. Before noon you're in his country.

Hop's mother and father like you a lot. Before long they're treating you like a new-found daughter. And Hop is treating you like a sister. Which is fine with you, because you've always wanted a brother — especially one your size.

You quickly find that Hop really likes adventures. He seems to attract them, the way a magnet attracts metal. He's even met a real-life ogre — that's where he got his seven-league boots.

"How would you like to come adventuring with me, little sister?" he asks.

That's an easy question to answer. "When do we start?" you say.

So the very next morning you and your new-found brother set off on a trip that may take you anywhere — anywhere at all.

THE END

"I think . . . yes, I think I'd like to find my real parents," you tell Wilma.

"Fine," she says. "But it won't be easy. And it will take you a very long time. You must go far, far to the south. You must go all the way to the Valley Most Deep."

"*Very* far?" you ask. Because you are so small, you know how long it takes you to get *anywhere* — let alone very far.

"Yes, but you must go, if you are to find your parents."

"Then I'll go," you say. "But how will I know when I'm there?"

"Ask," the witch answers. "Ask — and the Valley will tell you."

"Then I'll ask," you say. "Is there anything I should take with me?"

"Ah, you are a clever girl," says the witch, nodding. "Here."

She holds out two very large jewels. One is a rich, rich red color. The other is a bright, bright blue.

You clap your hands. "How pretty!"

"They're more than pretty." Now the witch's voice becomes very serious. "They're also magic. And you yourself must learn which *one* to use . . . and *when* to use it . . . and *how*."

Turn to **page 46.**

"Which one . . . when . . . how," you murmur. "Is there anything else I should know?"

"Clever again. Yes, there's one more thing. There is a very narrow path leading into the Valley Most Deep. It can only be found at noon on the longest day of the year. And then only for sixty seconds."

"One minute a year," you say. "That's not much time. But I'll be there."

The good witch Wilma looks at you for a moment. Then she smiles. "Yes, Thumbelina, I think you will. I really think you will. And Thumbelina, when you finally find your parents, say hello for me."

Say hello for me? What did the witch mean by that? But then you shrug and start walking south. You walk and you walk and you walk. Days pass. Then weeks. Then months. All the while everything around you is getting drier. It's also getting hotter. And the longest day grows closer and closer.

So you keep on walking no matter what, until finally you come to a land of many valleys. Is one of them mine? you wonder. How can I tell? Then you remember what the witch told you to do.

"Am I here?" you ask. "Is this the Valley Most Deep?"

Go on to the next page.

"Nay, nay, wee Thumbelina, nay;
   Go one league more, plus five;
But hurry — there's just one more day
   Until you must arrive."

You press on. Night falls and still you keep going. Then suddenly you see flames ahead of you — flames reaching up into the sky!

Far below is a deep, deep valley. "Am I here?" you ask once more. "Is this the Valley Most Deep?"

And an answer comes back to you:

"Yes, yes, wee Thumbelina, yes;
   You're here in time, my dear;
High noon will bring you full success —
   The pathway will appear."

But do you want to take that path? The valley is filled with huge fingers of flame. Flames that fill the whole night sky. How can you get through them? There seems to be no way. And yet . . . should you try?

If you decide you've come too far to go back, turn to **page 12.**

If you can't stand this heat any longer, turn back to **page 16** *and make another choice.*

48   You were right. Your kiss works. In the blink of an eye he turns into a Prince. A handsome Prince. Actually, a *very* handsome Prince.

There's just this one little thing — he's now about fifty times as big as you are. You forgot that people always are.

The frog's mother has changed, too. She's now a very lovely Queen. And her home has become a grand palace. Everything's changed, you think mournfully, everything except *me*. I'm just as small as ever.

The Prince seems to feel that this is your fault. "*Try* to get bigger," he says. "It isn't hard. *I* just did it."

Did I hear right? you think. *He* made himself bigger? *I* did it! But — why bring that up right now?

So you just say, "I'm afraid I can't."

"You could if you'd stop being so lazy and *try*," he says crossly. "Well, I suppose we'll have to send for the court magician. He'll get you up to size in a hurry."

Go on to the next page.

You look at this mean-tempered Prince. And you ask yourself — do I want to get big, just to please him? Do I want to go on knowing him at all?

But on the other hand, getting bigger might be quite an interesting adventure. So what do you choose?

If you'd rather stay the size you've always been, turn to **page 2.**

If you'll take a chance on getting enlarged, turn to **page 36.**

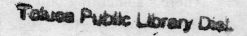

50   You know you won't get any help from the mouse or the mole. They don't like birds, dead *or* alive. But who else can you turn to?

You stay by the bird for a long time, wondering how to solve this problem. Then something very strange begins to happen. You are filled with a tingling feeling — a feeling that's somehow telling you what to do. And what it wants you to do is go outside.

Outside? you think. *Outside?* It's the middle of winter out there. It's very windy and very snowy and very cold. That's crazy!

But the tingling feeling gets stronger and stronger. And finally you obey it. You poke a hole in the top of the tunnel and crawl out.

It's cold, all right. You stand and shiver, wondering why you're there at all. But not for long. Soon you see a faraway figure in the clear night air. It's rushing toward you — moving fast — and getting closer by the second.

There's something odd about this figure. When people come closer to you, you expect them to seem bigger. But the nearer this one gets, the smaller he seems to be. Then he's standing right in front of you. And you see that he's tiny — hardly bigger than you are.

Go on to the next page.

"Hi," he says. "My name is Hop o' my Thumb. **51** But you can call me Hop, for short. Who are you?"

"Thumbelina," you tell him. "But I . . . I don't understand. How did you know I was here?"

"Oh, something told me," he answers. "It was a kind of tingling feeling. I always listen to things like that. Now, is there something I can do for you?"

"Yes," you say. "I do need help. A lot of it."

"I'm pretty good at that," says Hop. "What sort of help?"

You tell him about the swallow. "He's alive, but he's terribly weak. I've got to get him to a warm house."

"Why just a house?" Hop o' my Thumb asks. "Why not a warm country?"

"*Country?*"

"Sure," says Hop. "Anyway, let's start by getting him out of that tunnel."

It isn't easy, but you do it. Hop does most of the work. He's very strong. "All right," he says now, "off we go!"

"But how?" you ask.

Turn to **page 53.**

"Trust me," says Hop. Then he picks up the bird and puts him on his back. He tells you to climb on, too. The next moment all three of you are jumping across valleys and leaping over mountains.

"What's happening?!" you gasp.

Hop o' my Thumb laughs. "It's my seven-league boots," he explains. "They're magic. They go seven leagues in a single bound. And that's a long, long way."

"It certainly is," you answer, holding on tight. "But where are we going?"

"I told you. To a warm country. All the other birds of summer went there under their own power. Now we're helping your friend get there, too."

So that's where you go — all the way to the southern lands where birds fly for winter. You get there just as the sun is rising on a new day. You climb off Hop's back, and the two of you gently put the bird on the ground.

The swallow raises his head and flaps his wings a little. "Oh, thank you, thank you both," he whispers. "It feels so good to be warm. I'm much stronger already. Soon I'll be able to find my friends and really start living again. But right now I'm a little tired. . . ." The bird closes his eyes and drifts off to sleep.

Turn to **page 54.**

54   You and Hop sit nearby. "Now let's talk about you," says Hop o' my Thumb.

"Me?"

"Yes. I think you were wonderful — working so hard to save that bird. You're the kind of person I want to know better. Would you come back with me to my land? I'm sure you'd like it there."

But can you? You look at the swallow, sleeping nearby. He's still awfully weak. Can you leave him?

And besides, you haven't known Hop o' my Thumb for very long. Do you like him enough to go with him?

If you decide Hop O' my Thumb is fun and you want to get to know him better, turn to **page 44.**

If you think you should stay with the bird, turn to **page 29.**

You want to go home, all right, but which way
is home? You've never been in this part of the
world before. Oh, well, you think — I'll just start
walking and hope for the best.

After a while you come to a pond. And there —
sitting on the bank — is a frog. Oh, no! She looks
just like the frog who started all this trouble in
the first place!

You're about to turn and run when the frog
smiles at you and says, "So sit down, sit down.
We'll have a little chat."

And then you know she's a different frog. She
sounds nice, you think. But you still have one big
worry.

"You don't happen to have a son, do you? A
son you want to find a wife for?"

"A son I've got. But I wouldn't wish him on my
worst enemy. Believe me, you wouldn't like him.
Even a mother couldn't like him."

"Why? What's wrong with him?"

"Vain is what's wrong with him," the frog says.
"He thinks he's good-looking, is what's wrong with
him."

"Well, is he?"

"Good-looking?! He's a frog. How good-looking
can a frog be? Look at me — I'm a frog. Am I
good-looking?"

Turn to **page 56.**

"Well. . . ."

"Of course not," she says. "Nothing wrong with it — the world needs frogs, too. But good-looking? Ha! Anyway, let's talk about you for a while."

You tell the frog your story and she shakes her head. "After such a trip, anybody would be tired," she says. "You'd better come back to my place and rest up a little."

You go home with the frog. Her son is there. He's wearing a velvet jacket and a hat with a canary feather on it.

"It is indeed a pleasure to meet you," he says. "I say, you're not bad-looking. No, not bad-looking at all. Not as marvelous-looking as I am, of course — who could be? But not at all bad."

You look at his mother, who shrugs. "He talks that way all the time. I warned you, remember."

"Pay no attention to Mother," he says. "She thinks I'm vain. But how could I be vain when I'm so wonderful? Naturally, I'm better-looking than she is. I'm adopted, you know."

Later, while you're resting, you think about those two frogs. The mother is so nice, and the son is so . . . well, weird. And the way he talks! He sounds like a prince, or something.

Go on to the next page.

And then you begin to wonder. Could he be . . . yes, could he be under some kind of a spell? Could he really be a Prince who's been turned into a frog? You've heard about that sort of thing. And he did say he was adopted. . . .

Well, if he is under a spell, there's only one cure. You've read about it in lots of fairy tales. You have to kiss him. If there's a spell, that should break it. Why not give it a try?

So you walk up to the frog and kiss him solidly, right in the middle of his frog-green forehead. Then you stand back to see what happens.

If your kiss doesn't work, turn to **page 4.**

But if it does, turn to **page 48.**

58   You climb on the swallow's back, and he takes off. Soon you're flying over valleys and fields and forests and great seas. The bird soars over a high, high mountain range. The air is very cold up there, but you creep under his soft feathers and they warm you like a blanket.

Then you leave the mountains behind, and the air grows warmer. You look down and see a bright, beautiful land.

"Are we there?" you ask.

"Almost," says the swallow.

You keep flying south until you see a great white palace ahead. "That's where I live," the swallow tells you. "I have a nest high up under the roof. But I think you'd be happier living in the flower garden below."

The swallow swoops down and lands near a lovely white flower. You blink with surprise, for sitting on it is a man almost as small as you are. He has wings that glisten like diamonds, and a golden crown on his head.

"Who is he?" you whisper.

"He's the spirit of the flower," the swallow explains to you. "Every flower here has one, but he's the King of them all. Would you like to meet him?"

Go on to the next page.

"Oh, please," you say, for he's the handsomest man you've ever seen.

So the bird introduces you and then flies away. The two of you sit down by his flower and begin to talk. And while you talk, you're thinking about the others you've just met. First, there was the frog's slimy son. Then there was the fickle June bug. Finally, there was the smug mole.

This man is certainly nicer and handsomer than all three of *them* put together, you think.

The King feels the same way about you. Now he holds out his crown and says, "Will you marry me? Will you be Queen of all the flowers?"

"Oh, yes!" you tell him. "I will."

The very next day you are married. And the small spirit people who live in the other flowers bring you presents. The grandest present of all is a pair of glistening wings, just like the ones the King has.

"Now you can fly with me wherever I go," he says. And that's just what you do. Often the two of you fly off alone. But sometimes a friend comes along. Your very best friend, in fact. Who? Why, the swallow, of course.

THE END

60   There's a hot blast of fire as the bird goes screaming by over your head — then it is gone. You're safe. But for how long? Surely the bird will come back for another try.

No, there's no time to lose. You've got to keep going as fast as you can. So you struggle on, deeper into the valley. Then you see a castle in the distance. Fires burn all around it, almost up to the stone walls. But you use your blue stone to beat back the flames until you get to the front door.

You go inside. The castle is very large, and very hot, and very, very dry. Every room is furnished. The beds are made, the curtains are clean, the table is set for dinner. But no one is there.

You wander from room to room. Most of them are bright with the dancing flames outside. Then you come to a small inner room which is almost dark. In it is a glass case. And in the case are two dried-up flowers.

Flowers, you think. I came from a flower. My adoptive mother said so. Could these be. . . .

Turn to **page 62.**

62   You open the glass case, and then you know. Lying inside one of the flowers is a man, as small as you are. Lying inside the other is a woman. They are your real parents. And they're as dried-up as everything else in this house.

Now I'll never know them, you think. I've come all this way, to find out they're dead.

This makes you so sad you begin to cry. One of your tears falls on the dried-up man. Another falls on the woman.

You can't bear to look at them any more, and you turn to leave. But then a voice behind you says, "Thank you . . . thank you for your tears."

You spin around, and there are your mother and father. They're smiling at you and holding out their arms.

"You're alive!" you cry, as you hug them. "But *how*?"

"Your loving tears have brought us back to life," says your father.

"But I don't understand. What happened to you?"

"An evil witch put us under a spell, many years ago," your mother tells you. "She put us in those flowers. Then she filled our whole valley with fire."

Go on to the next page.

"How did *I* escape?" you ask.

"You didn't. The witch turned you into a seed. But then Amadeus picked you up and flew you out to safety."

"Amadeus?"

"He was our bluebird," your mother continues. "He came back and tried to rescue us, too. But he was too late."

You look around with a shiver. "Where is the witch now? Could she come back?"

"She might," says your father unhappily. "She usually takes the form of a bird — a bird with feathers of flame."

"I've already met her!" you cry. "She tried to kill me."

"Then we must leave — leave at once!"

"But we can't," you tell them. "The path is only open one minute a year."

"We don't need the path," your father says. "Amadeus will carry us over the mountains."

He is pointing across the room. You look and see a bird lying in the corner. "Him? How can he help us? He's dead!"

"No," says your mother. "Not dead — just dried-up, as we were."

Turn to **page 64.**

64   Now she touches your cheek and finds a single tear there. She touches Amadeus with it. And in an instant he's alive and spreading his wings.

"Come," says your father. "There's no time to lose." The three of you climb onto the bluebird's back. In a moment, you are flying far above the burning valley.

But soon your father turns and shouts, "There's the witch! And she's closing in fast! I'm afraid we're not going to make it!"

If you suddenly think of a way to fight the witch, turn to **page 10.**

If you can't, maybe you'd better turn back to **page 12** *and make another choice.*

You feel a terrible burning as the bird's claws close on you. Desperately you try to fight it off. But the bird is too strong. It's about to fly off — with you in its grasp!

Then you think of your jewel. You twist around and thrust it toward the bird.

A beam of blue light shoots out from the jewel. It hits the bird right between the eyes. There's a loud *squawk!* and the bird falls at your feet.

It lands with a heavy clunk. And no wonder. It's been turned to solid stone. Solid *blue* stone — as blue as the jewel in your hand.

Suddenly you feel a cool breeze. When you look up, you see that the fires have gone. All across the valley there's not a flame to be seen. Flowers and grass are growing everywhere.

With a much lighter heart, you start on your way once more. You haven't gone far when you notice that something else is changing. You! With each step you're getting bigger. Soon you're the same height as other people. You are Thumbelina no more.

Turn to **page 66.**

66   At last you see a castle in the distance. It stands on top of a hill. All around it are flower gardens, and to one side is a blue, blue lake.

Then you notice two people standing in front of the castle. They are both wearing crowns on their heads. They must be the King and Queen of this place, you think.

"Maia!" they cry as you draw near. "Oh, Maia, it *is* you. We knew it must be!"

"Maia?" you say. "Is . . . is that my name?"

"Yes! And you are our daughter. The daughter we lost so long ago!" They rush forward and hug you.

Your parents. You don't remember ever seeing them. But these are your long-lost parents at last!

"We knew you would come back and save us one day," says your mother, the Queen.

"Save you? How? What must I do?"

They laugh. "I'm sure you've already done it, my dear," says your father, the King. "Somehow you have lifted the spell a wicked witch put on us — or the fires would not have gone out."

You show them the blue jewel. "I stopped a fiery bird with this. The bird turned to stone and the fires went out."

Go on to the next page.

"Ah," the King says. "That bird was the evil witch — the one who put us under the spell and made us very tiny. Then she took our whole valley away from us. She made it into a place of fire and death."

"But there's one thing I don't understand," you say. "How did we get separated in the first place?"

Your mother explains. "That was the witch again. You were the first person she threatened."

"Me? Why me?"

"Wicked witches never like babies," she says. "Anyway, a good witch was also visiting the valley. Her name was — "

"I know," you say. "Wilma!"

"Yes. So Wilma shrank you to the size of a seed and then smuggled you out of the valley in her pocket."

You smile. You know what happened next to that seed.

But all that's in the past. The next day your mother and father put a lovely crown on your head. Set in the very middle of it is your blue jewel.

And you know that from now on the three of you — your father, the King; your mother, the Queen; and you, Princess Maia — will live happily ever after together in the Valley Most Deep.

THE END

You sleep peacefully through the rest of the night. But as soon as you open your eyes in the morning, you know something is terribly wrong. Your walnut-shell bed is sitting on a lily pad in the middle of a river — with you still in it. And you can't swim!

This makes you very unhappy — so unhappy that you start to cry. A few minutes later something happens to make you even more unhappy. The frog comes back. And there's another frog with her.

"This is my son," she tells you. "Isn't he handsome?"

Handsome? you think.

"Before the day is over the two of you will be married," continues the proud mother. "Then you'll live happily ever after in a nice cozy mud bank. Won't that be fun?"

Fun? you think.

Now the frog turns to her son. "Say something to the pretty girl, son," she says.

"Rad-it! Rad-it!" he croaks happily. Then off they swim.

Oh, what am I going to do? you think. Whatever is going to become of me?

Go on to the next page.

You begin to cry again. Everything looks so
hopeless. But a fish under the water has heard
the whole thing. Now he dives down and chews
through the stem of your lily pad. And you go
floating off down the river.

"Good-bye — and good luck!" he calls after
you.

Turn to **page 70.**

70　　The tears dry on your face. You start to hum a happy song. For the day is warm. The sun is bright. And with each passing second the current is carrying you farther and farther from those two frogs.

But then a June bug flies past. He sees you on your lily pad. He picks you up and carries you into the branches of a tall tree.

"How pretty you are," he says. "Here, have some honey I was saving for lunch. Then let's get married."

Before you can say anything to this sudden offer, some other June bugs arrive. And they don't agree with your June bug at all.

"Why, she only has two legs," one of them says.

"Yes, and where are her feelers?"

"*Or* her wings!" a third complains. "We don't want *her* marrying into our family!"

Then all together they say, "How ugly she is! Ugly! Ugly! Ugly!"

Go on to the next page.

Your June bug looks at you with new eyes. He certainly doesn't want to be different from the others. So he picks you up and carries you down to the ground. He leaves you there, sitting under a daisy in the middle of a big meadow.

What do you do now?

If you think you'd like to stay where you are for a while, turn to **page 19.**

If you'd rather try to find your way back home, turn to **page 55.**

You're not strong enough to crack that pillar of ice — not nearly. But there might be another way . . . your red jewel.

You touch the icy column with it. And once more it serves you well. There is a sizzling noise, like water boiling. Steam begins to rise. Finally you hear a *drip, drip, dripping* sound as the pillar starts to melt.

A few minutes later, it's gone. All that's left is a puddle on the floor of the cave. And standing in the puddle is a young man.

He's very tall — taller than anyone you've ever seen. And he's very handsome. But he's also as still and white as a statue. He looks very dead. Is there anything you can do to save him?

You begin to get a feeling — almost like a voice without words. It seems to be telling you that you must touch his closed eyes with your red jewel.

But *how*? you think. I don't even come up to his ankle. How can I get all the way up to his eyes? It's impossible!

Still, you know you've got to try. You've spent all these months — come all this way — you're not going to give up now. And so you start climbing.

Go on to the next page.

It's the hardest thing you've ever done in your life. You think you're never going to make it. It's too high. It's too hard. It's too dangerous. But at last — somehow — you're there. And you touch his eyes with your magic jewel.

The tall, tall man opens his eyes. He smiles and says, "Who . . . who are you?"

Quickly you tell him all about yourself . . . the good witch Wanda . . . the Quest she has sent you on . . . and the magic red jewel. "It's thanks to the jewel," you say, "that you're free of that pillar of ice."

"No, Thumbelina," the young man answers. "It's thanks to *you*. For you were the one who cared enough to keep on going when you were cold and tired and afraid. And for that I thank you from the bottom of my heart."

"You're very welcome, sir."

"Call me Manfred," he says. "But come, let's get out of this cold, cold cave."

You think this is a good idea. So the young man sets off. It took you three hours to get into the cave — he gets you out in three minutes.

Once you're outside, he looks at you and says, "Now I can go home. Would you like to come with me?"

Turn to **page 74.**

"Yes, I'd like to," you say.

Manfred spreads his cape and leaps into the air. In an instant, the two of you are flying over the mountaintops.

When he sees the surprised look on your face he says, "I should have told you. I'm something of a magician. And flying is so much easier than walking, don't you think?"

"But if you're a magician, how did. . . ?"

"How did I get in that pillar of ice?"

You nod.

"Well, I made an enemy of a very evil witch — I saved someone she tried to put a spell on. Then one day she found me when I was taking a nap. Because I was asleep, I couldn't protect myself against her magic. That's when she froze me in the ice. Forever, she thought. And it would have been, if you hadn't come."

The magic cape zooms you over hills and valleys and oceans. Now, as the sky is growing light in the east, you swoop down and land in front of a very large house.

You go inside with him and continue to talk. You talk for the rest of the day. By evening, you feel as though you've known Manfred for years. No, it's more than that. By now you know that you have met the man you're going to love.

Go on to the next page.

He feels the same about you. There's only one thing that bothers you both — the difference in your sizes.

"Thumbelina," he says at last, "if I made myself as small as you — would you marry me?"

"You'd do that for me? You'd give up all the wonderful things in your world — for me?"

"Yes," Manfred answers simply. "I would. Will you let me do it, Thumbelina?"

You shake your head. "No, Manfred," you tell him. "I like being small. But it can be very lonely. I don't think you'd be happy like this."

"Well," he says, "will you let me use my magic to make *you* grow bigger?"

You think about it for a few minutes. Then you smile. "Yes, I'd like that."

And that's what happens. Manfred puts a finger on top of your head. He says some magic words. And in the blink of an eye, you're almost as tall as he is.

You and Manfred don't settle down. You still have your magic jewels, and he has his magic powers. So the two of you decide to go on more Quests. And who knows what exciting adventures lie ahead — for the two of you together?

THE END

Did you know that the story of *Thumbelina*, written by Hans Christian Andersen more than a hundred years ago, is in this book? If you're not sure which it is, here's how to find it:

Start on **page 1**, and when you get to the choice at the end of the page, turn to **page 68**.

Read **pages 68, 69, 70, and 71**, then turn to **page 19**.

Read **pages 19, 20, 21, 22, and 23**, then turn to **page 41**.

Read **pages 41, 42, and 43**, then turn to **page 58**.

Read **pages 58 and 59**.

When you get to "The End" on the bottom of **page 59**, you've finished the real story of *Thumbelina*.